ABBY, THE WONDER DOG
AND HER
WARRIOR PRINCESS

by
Melanie Ewbank

Illustrated by Samuel Jack

Climbing Angel Publishing

Abby, the Wonder Dog and her Warrior Princess
by Melanie Ewbank

Illustrated by Samuel Jack

International Children's Bible:
(ICB) The Holy Bible, International Children's Bible® Copyright© 1986, 1988, 1999, 2015 by Tommy Nelson™, a division of Thomas Nelson.

Published in 2022 by:
Climbing Angel Publishing
PO Box 32381
Knoxville, Tennessee 37930
www.ClimbingAngel.com

First Edition September 2022
Printed in the United States of America

Cover & Interior design by Climbing Angel Publishing

ISBN: 978-1-956218-22-0

*For all **Wonder Dogs** everywhere
(whether official or unofficial) who love unconditionally,
who selflessly serve to protect, to alert, and to comfort—
and for my very own **Warrior Princess**, her Mama, and
her Papa. You are the bravest people I know.*

Abby, the Wonder Dog

and her
Warrior Princess

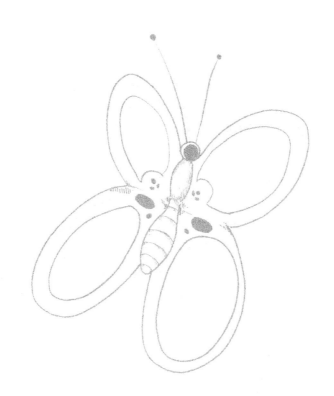

1

Commmmpannnnyyyy!

Sunday

What a great day! For now, at least.

Even though Papa's gear is by the front door, and that means he's leaving for a very long time. A very, very, verrry long time. And even though this Friday will be a very scary day, and Papa won't be here to give hugs. Even though with all that, for now, we're happy.

We have company! Mama is having a few friends over to wish Papa bon voyage. I don't know what that means, I just know that I'm not wearing my special vest. And that means I can be petted by the people. When my vest is on, I'm working. When I'm working, my job is to keep my eyes open, my ears perked, my mind alert, and my heart tuned into my handler.

See, I'm a service dog. When I'm working, I cannot have distractions. But today, the vest is off, and I am busy getting plenty distracted! I'm so excited that I'm already ahead of myself. Usually, I'm calm, focused, and level-headed. I have to be. But Mama said, "Free dog," and that means I am free to be a dog!

We need an introduction. Introductions are very important to dogs. But *our* kind of introductions make humans uncomfortable, so we can skip that. My name is Abby. I'm a Labradoodle. I work for Savannah.

Mama and Papa call her "Savannah Warrior Princess" or "Savanner-Danner-Doo," but I just call her "MH." That's short for "My Handler." That means she is the person I'm here to serve and protect. MH is also short for "My Hero" because Savannah is the bravest person I know.

Savannah is eight years old. I am two years old. She's smart. I'm smart. She doesn't talk much, but boy, she sure says a lot! And me? I'm a dog. Oh, you already know that.

Wait. What was I going to tell you? Let's see. Great day, no vest, company, petted by the people, distractions. Oh, right! Herkimer the Camel. MH throws Herkimer, the stuffed toy camel, out the door of her room for me to chase. Camels are not aerodynamic. That means the camel doesn't fly so well. He wobbles through the air.

"Woo hoo! Good arm!" Papa says. I've also heard MH's coach say that to her when she plays that game. You know, the game where they whack the ball with a stick, then run around in a circle. What's the point of that? I mean, I understand running in circles, but why isn't everyone chasing that ball?

Wait. What was I going to tell you? Let's see. Herkimer the Camel, Warrior Princess, good arm. Oh, right! Playing possum. I race down the hall as fast as my legs will take me.

"Get that camel!" Papa calls out as MH giggles.

Herkimer bounces once, and I grab him mid-air. I streak through the kitchen and round the corner, feet skidding, toenails digging in for traction. I'm bounding toward the living room with thoughts of a good back scratch from one of our visitors. I can't get a good back scratch when I'm wearing my special vest.

Wait. What was I going to tell you? Let's see. Herkimer the Camel, Warrior Princess, good arm, playing possum, bounding, back scratch. Oh, right! Smart cookie.

From nowhere, Mama appears, blocking my path. *Abort! Abort!* I tell my legs, but I'm scrambling for a foothold, and I fail. I flop on my belly,

feet splayed out to my sides, and slide to a stop at Mama's feet. I say to myself, *Stay still, don't blink, don't breathe. She might not see me if I don't move and play possum.*

"Abby," Mama says. And just like that, I'm betrayed by my tail. Wag, wag, wag it goes.

I scooch myself to a sitting position so I can give Mama my best *puppy-dog-eyes* look. I tilt my head one way, then the other for maximum effect.

"Awwww!" Mama says.

Yes! I think to myself. *Now I have her in the palm of my hand.*

"Take that stuffy back to your room, please," Mama adds.

Drat! Dogs don't have palms or hands. Mama is a smart cookie. I stand. I turn. I hang my head and slowly make my way back down the hall.

A squeal of laughter flies out to meet me. This happy sound is my favorite. I like it even more than the sound of kibble hitting my food dish, and that is a fantastic sound! I have sensitive ears, and so does MH. Too many sounds at once or loud, surprising sounds make her very anxious. One of my jobs is to help her feel better. It's a great job. It's a hugging job!

Wait. What was I going to tell you? Let's see. Herkimer the Camel, Warrior Princess, good arm, playing possum, bounding, back scratch, smart cookie. Oh, right! Savanner-Danner-Doo. I dash into the room to find Papa on all fours. MH is riding on Papa's back like a horse.

"Where to, my lady?" he asks. "You ready to join the party?"

"Almost." She climbs off his back and sits on the floor. I can tell she's sad. I lie next to her and put my head on her lap. "I'm sorry, Papa," she whispers.

Papa sits beside her. "For what, Princess?"

"For taking your brave."

"But we share my brave! I always have extra brave for you."

"But you need all of your brave to be a good soldier."

"Didn't I tell you? It grows back."

"It does?!"

"Well, sure. Every night when I tuck you in, and we say our prayers, all my brave fills to the tippy top of me. I never run out."

"But you won't be here to tuck me in. How can it fill to the tippy top of you?"

"It gets supercharged when we video chat. In fact, you give me so much brave I have extra to share with my squad."

"Really?"

"Yes, really. Now, are you ready to party?"

She smiles and bobs her head up and down as she climbs on Papa's back. "Go, my trusty steed!" MH pretends to snap the reigns.

On hands and knees, Papa moves through the house, sometimes at a smooth gait and sometimes at a bumpy canter. This sends MH into fits of giggles. I follow close behind, ready to work if I need to, even though I'm not wearing my vest. When we arrive at the living room, I sit by Mama as MH dismounts.

Papa announces, "Presenting her Royal Highness, The Warrior Princess, Savanner-Danner-Doo!"

As Papa and MH rejoin the party, the guests softly cheer and clap so they don't make much noise. MH takes a regal bow. Papa sits on the floor with his arms open wide, and she plunks down into her comfy "Papa" throne. She sits up very tall and places her arms on top of his.

Mama scratches my back in long strokes with one hand while rubbing my ears with the other. Tomorrow when Papa leaves, we all will use up a lot of brave. But today is a great day.

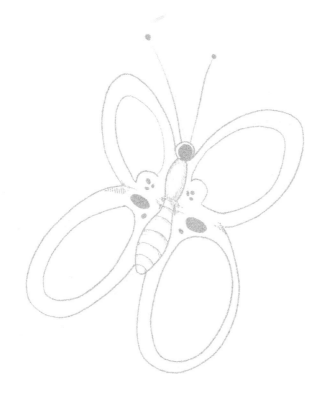

2

Rules are for Safety

Monday

MH and I are sitting in the blanket fort Papa made before he left this morning. She is reading one of the notes he clipped to a string of twinkle lights. She started the day feeling sad, but now she's smiling.

Ding dong.

Oh, boy! Someone is at the door! I think to myself.

MH bolts for the stairs, with me on her heels. She flings her leg over the banister and then glances back at Mama.

"Careful!" Mama calls as MH laughs.

"Let's goooooooo," MH screams as she slides all the way to the bottom. I hurry down the stairs to meet her. She jumps off the railing and heads for the door.

"Wait!" Mama says, "What's the rule?"

"'See who it is first,'" MH says, leaning into the door.

Once Mama joins us, MH drops to her knees and plants her face against the mail slot. She pushes it open and peers out.

I stick my nose close to MH's face and take a good sniff. *It's Mary, our letter carrier!*

"Mail call!" Mary yells.

"Mail call!" MH excitedly repeats as a stack of mail is pushed through the slot. "Thank you, Mary," MH yells through the opening as she takes the letters. The mail slot slaps closed.

"Knock, knock," Mary calls out.

"Who's there," MH answers with a giggle.

"Package for Savanner-Danner-Doo."

"That's me!" MH leaps to her feet and drops the stack of mail on the floor. She grabs the doorknob in one hand and the deadbolt lock in the other. "Okay, Mama?" she asks.

"Okay," Mama answers, picking up the scattered mail.

MH flings the door open wide. Mary holds a package out to MH with a happy smile.

"Thank you!" MH squeals.

"You're welcome! See you tomorrow Savanner-Danner-Doo!" Mary gives a wave and then closes the door.

MH rushes into the kitchen, putting her package on the counter.

"Watch the stove. It's hot!" Mama calls out.

MH yanks a drawer open and pulls something sharp out of it.

"Wait, wait," Mama says, "What's the rule?"

MH doesn't wait. Mama rounds the corner into the kitchen.

"Savannah, the rule is to wait for me. Put that knife down right now, please, and step away from the stove."

"It's cookies, Mama! From Grandma!" MH quickly places the sharp thing onto the package and pulls it across. She yelps and holds up her wounded hand. Blood comes out of it where she cut herself. MH looks at her hand and panics. Her knees begin to shake as she shouts, "No, no! No hospital! Please, Mama!"

Mama steps behind MH, and they slowly sink to the floor together. I crawl into MH's lap and nudge her face with my nose. I press my body against hers. I can feel her take a deep breath. She gives me a squeeze to tell me she is okay.

"May I touch your hand?" Mama asks. MH nods and holds it out for inspection. "It's just a little cut. I think we can bandage you up right here."

"At home? No doctor?"

"Not today," Mama says as she stands. "Are you okay here with Abby while I get a bandage?"

"Yes, Mama. I'll say my Psalms."

"Perfect."

"'I have angels in charge to watch over me wherever I am. Even if you're not with me. Even when Daddy's not here.'"

"That's right." Mama sighs and starts down the hall. "I'll be right back."

"I'm in trouble, Abby," MH whispers sadly. "Rules are for safety, and I didn't follow the rules. I hurt myself."

I lay my head against MH's chest.

Mama is back in a flash and sits on the floor again. "Can you think of something we can do differently next time we get a package?" Mama asks as she carefully cleans the fresh cut.

"'Wait for Mama to be safe.'"

"Yes. 'Wait for Mama to be safe.' You really scared me, Savannah. You were much too close to that hot stove."

"But —"

"And we need to practice where to put your hands when using sharp things. Kitchen knives are not for opening boxes."

"Oh, I didn't know. Sorry, I scared you."

"Thank you," Mama says.

"I didn't use up too much brave, Mama. I promise. I bet Papa won't even notice."

"I bet you're right."

"I might need some tonight, though. Can I call Papa tonight?" MH asks.

"He's on a plane with his squad, remember? He'll call us tomorrow night."

"Can I sleep with Abby in Papa's spot tonight?" MH pleads, giving Mama her best *puppy-dog-eyes* look that she learned from me. It is very effective.

"Yes, you may. Now, let's get you bandaged, then we'll see if any of Grandma's cookies can be saved!"

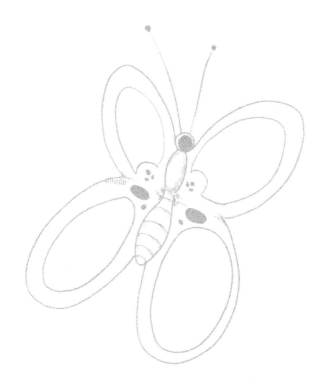

3

Housekeeping

 Tuesday

"Savannah, come in here and pick your toys up off the floor, please," Mama calls out from the living room for the second time.

"I like where they are!" MH calls back from her room.

"I'm going to run the vacuum in here, and I'm going to keep anything I have to bend over and pick up off this floor!"

"No, Mama! Those are mine!"

"They're about to be mine!"

MH runs into the living room with me close on her heels. She scoops her toys up off the floor and tosses them onto the couch. Herkimer the Camel lands hump-side down on a rubber snake. Two plastic pigs bounce like they're dancing. MH grins. "Okay, Mama, all clean!" MH yells as she runs down the hall to her room. "Headphones on, Mama!" MH makes sure her headphones only cover one ear.

Mama turns on the vacuum. Mama turns off the vacuum. "Savannah Marie!" she calls. That's Mama-speak for 'get your rear in gear and appear in here right now!'

MH looks at me with wide eyes, then says, "C'mon, Abby. You go first!" I stay very still and look away.

"Abigail Fuzzface!" MH says to me with her hands firmly on her hips.

I run down the hall. MH follows. I stop in the doorway to the living room. MH runs past me, giggling.

"Just joking, Mama! I'll put these toys in my room!" MH looks back at me with a sneaky grin. She picks up the rubber snake, then shoves it between the couch cushions. "Shhhhh," she whispers to me. She grabs Herkimer the Camel and the two pigs, then races down the hall to her bedroom. "Stay, Abby," she shouts to me as she rushes past.

Mama turns on the vacuum and pushes it around in front of the couch. MH quietly tiptoes up behind me and crouches. She holds Mama's phone up in the air. *When did she get the phone,* I wonder?

Mama shuts off the vacuum. She then picks up a couch cushion, and the rubber snake flies high in the air. It wriggles past Mama's face as if it has come to life, then bounces on the floor.

"Aaaaaaaaaaaahhhhhh!" Mama screams as she scrambles away from the snake.

MH collapses into a fit of giggles, managing to snort out, "Oops, I forgot one!"

"You stinker!" Mama grins. "Is that my phone? Did you record that?!"

"You are not very brave today, Mama!" MH squeals with delight as she races down the hall. "I'm showing this to Papa when he calls tomorrow!"

Mama listens to MH's contagious giggles as they disappear behind the bedroom door. Mama stands in front of me and takes my face into her hands. "Isn't that the best sound ever?" she asks, then runs down the hall after MH. "I'm gonna get you, Savanner-Danner-Doo!"

I agree completely—*MH's happy squeals and giggles really are the best sound ever!* I turn and bolt down the hall, sprinting after Mama.

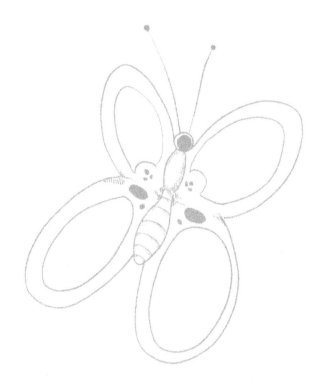

4

Always Ask

 *Wednesday*

"Savannah," the nurse calls out.

Mama stands, but MH doesn't move. "Come on. Time to go in," Mama says. "Abby, up."

I stand and push against MH's leg. She doesn't move. I turn to face her and nudge her knee with my nose. Nudge, nudge, nudge. Mama walks toward the nurse, who holds the door open.

MH takes my leash in her hand and stands. She slowly walks to Mama. "I don't want to," she says.

"I know. It's just a quick check-in before Friday."

"No shots!" MH insists.

"No shots," the nurse repeats. "I promise. Just looking and listening and maybe taking your temperature."

MH turns and skips down the hall, singing, "This little light of mine, I'm gonna let it shine, let it shine, let it shine." She hops up on the table. "Let it shiiiiine!" She finishes with a flourish. Her feet dangle. She swings them back and forth, back and forth. MH starts to get anxious, waiting for the nurse to come in. She covers her ears, squeezes her eyes shut, and sings to herself. Mama calls it stimming. This is one of the ways MH gets anxiety out of her body. This time she sings her favorite song about her favorite food. "Cheese, cheese, a stick of cheese! I would like some cheddar, please!" MH repeats her cheese song over and over, swinging her legs, eyes closed, ears covered.

Someone taps on the door. "Come in," Mama says.

"Good morning, Savannah," a cheery nurse says with a smile.

MH scrunches her face and presses her hands tighter against her ears. She sings a little louder. "Cheese, cheese, a stick of cheese! I would like some cheddar, please!"

I press my head against her legs, hoping to help.

The nurse smiles at Mama, then puts something in her ears so she can hear MH's body. "I'm going to listen to her chest," she tells Mama. "We need to get her vitals today before the MRI on Friday."

The cheery nurse turns to MH, whose eyes are squeezed tightly shut and whose ears are covered.

"Wait!" Mama says too late, as the cheery nurse puts her hand on MH's back and touches the listening thing to MH's chest.

MH shrieks and jumps off the table. I stand as MH flies into Mama's lap and buries her head in Mama's chest.

This scares the cheery nurse. "I'm sorry! I'm so sorry, Savannah."

"No! NO, NO, NO!" MH cries out.

I push my head under MH's arm. I nudge her with my nose.

"We're going to need a minute," Mama says quietly to the nurse.

"Of course," she answers as she backs out of the room. "I'm so sorry, Savannah. I didn't mean to scare you." The nurse shuts the door.

I nudge MH's hand again with my nose. She begins to lightly scratch me between my ears. After a moment, she quiets.

"I was not ready, Mama," MH mumbles into Mama's chest.

"No, you were not."

MH lifts her head. "I didn't know she was there 'cuz I was singing my cheese song."

"I know! I heard you. What a good job you did with self-care!"

"But I ruined it."

"It's not ruined. It's just on pause. The cheese song is ready and waiting to be sung."

"I can't, Mama."

"Did you forget how it goes?"

"No, I could never!"

"Think you can get back up on the table and sing your song?"

"Only with Abby."

"Abby knows the cheese song?"

"No, silly! Abby doesn't sing!" MH laughs and rolls her eyes.

MH slides off Mama's lap and moves to the table. The paper crinkles as MH tries to straighten it, then she crawls back up and sits, feet dangling.

"Abby, hug," she says. "This is so hard, Mama."

I stand on my hind legs and put my front paws around her waist. She holds my head in her hands and rubs my cheeks. There is a tap, tap, tap sound on the door. Mama looks at MH.

"If you're ready, you can answer," she says.

"Who's there?" MH asks.

The nurse cracks the door open and sticks her head through. "I'm very, very sorry, Savannah," she says softly. "May I come in?"

"Yes, but no surprises," MH answers.

"No surprises," repeats the nurse.

"Always ask before touching," MH says. "Even Mama has to. Everyone. Always ask first."

"Thank you for reminding me. I will always ask first. Everything checks out perfectly for your test on Friday, so you are free to go."

As we walk to the car, Mama's phone makes the noise that means Papa is calling. Mama hands the phone to MH and unlocks the car. MH gets in and puts on her seatbelt.

"Hi, Papa! I used a bunch of brave today! But I sang the cheese song, so there's still some left for you!"

"You saved me some cheese? Wow! Thank you!" Papa jokes.

"No way, Papa. You know I don't share cheese!"

Papa laughs. Mama starts the car but doesn't drive. She looks in the rear-view mirror at MH and smiles a sad smile.

"Listen," Papa says. "I may not get to call you tomorrow, and I want you to have sweet dreams before your big day on Friday, so I have a little surprise. You ready?"

"A nice surprise?"

"Of course, it's a nice surprise, silly!"

"Is it cheese?"

"Of course, it's cheese! Ready, squad?"

Papa's squad gathers in front of his computer screen. "Ready, sir!"

"Company, sing!" Papa barks his order, and they all join in.

"Clap your hands and slap your knees. Warrior Princess loves some cheese. There's lots of brave inside her tank. But we put more in her brave bank. She's tough and strong. She'll do her best. We've got her back while she takes this test. And once she's done, Mama, if you please. Get that girl a stick of cheese!"

"Company dismissed!" Papa barely barks out before he snort-laughs.

MH joins in with a laugh that comes from down in her belly. Mama makes laughing noises, but they're a little sad sounding. She wipes her eyes and puts the car in gear.

"Matthew, Chapter 6, Verse 34," Mama whispers. She takes a deep breath in. Then slowly, lets it out, along with the sad. "Right, Abby? Can't worry about tomorrow. Today's trouble is enough." Then she smiles.

Boy, I think. *That's even more powerful than the cheese song.*

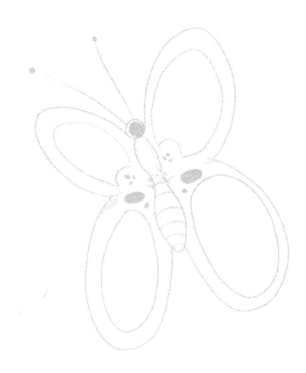

5

One Big Reason I'm Here

Thursday

MH needs to sit down right now. Right now!

"Sit!" I bark loudly as I block her with my body. Her eyes glaze over, her knees buckle, and I'm ready for what always comes next. She reaches out for me as she tumbles forward. I cushion her landing and crawl out from underneath, nudging her into a safe position on her side. I lift my head high and bark loud and sharp, "Mama! Mama! Mama!"

Mama is in the room she hates the most. The one with mounds of clothes and the machine that makes them bubble. I hear her singing to the music, but the words don't match the ones in the song. "Hello, little socks, where are your mates—?"

"Mama! Mama! Mama," I bark again as I move to MH's head so I can lick her face.

"Abby?!" Mama calls from downstairs.

I lift my head high again and bark my answer.

Mama rushes up the stairs and into the room. MH's body begins to calm and settle. Mama stands by as I lick MH's face until she reaches up for me and rolls onto her back. Mama lies down on one side of MH, and I move to the other, as we sandwich her between us. MH wraps her arm around my neck as I lay my head on her chest.

Mama and I stay there. We are very still, just listening to MH breathe. We stay there for a long, long time.

"Mama," MH whispers, breaking the silence.

"Yes, baby?"

"Why does my body do that to me?"

"I don't know, precious. We're trying to find out."

"At the doctor?"

"Yes, at the doctor."

"To look at my brain?"

"Yes."

"In the tube?"

"Yes."

"I *have* to go?"

"Unless you can pop your brain out of your noggin, baby girl. Yes, you *have* to go."

MH smiles. "If Papa comes, and you come, and Abby comes, maybe I can be brave enough."

"Well, Papa's brave is yours while he's away."

"Papa needs his brave, Mama. He needs all of it."

"Papa has enough brave for all of us, don't you worry. Besides, I think you've got all the brave you need."

"I used a lot today."

"Have you ever run out?

"I don't think so."

"Remember our Matthew, Chapter 6, Verse 34?"

"Yes, Mama. Don't worry about tomorrow."

"Amen."

6

No Biting

Friday

MH is so brave. She is going into the tube today.

The tube is very loud and almost too small for her. I can't be in the tube room with MH. It's not safe for me or Mama, so Mama and I will sit in this room with the window.

The lady-behind-the-desk doesn't want me in this room either. Mama knows the rules, though. Mama knows a trick called "Supervisor."

"Thank you," Mama says to the lady-behind-the-desk. "Now, may I please speak with your Supervisor?" Mama uses the "Supervisor" trick twice more before I am allowed to stay.

I wish there were earplugs for dogs. There are hats, and sweaters, and booties for dogs. But no earplugs. Today the tube is supposed to be quieter, though.

Sometimes they give MH sleepy medicine, so she's not scared to do something scary. But the sleepy medicine makes her sick. Today MH is scared, but Mama says she should try going into the tube without the sleepy medicine. Mama says, "Twenty minutes in the tube, *scared*, might be better than two days with a sick tummy."

We stand in the doorway and stare at the tube. MH holds my leash in one hand and Mama's hand in the other. She is very scared. She mumbles over and over again, "'For he will command his angels concerning you to guard you in all your ways.'"

"Ready?" the lady-in-the-tube-room asks cheerfully. She then steps toward MH.

MH is not ready. I can feel it. I step between MH and the lady-in-the-tube-room. I look up at Mama. MH wraps her arms around my neck and squeezes.

"Just one more moment," Mama says quietly to the lady-in-the-tube-room.

"Of course. Take as much time as you need," she replies. "When you're ready, you can choose your movie."

"Movie?" MH asks.

"Why, yes. You get to watch a movie. With special headphones."

"*Tweedle Dee and Tweedle Dum*?" MH asks.

Mama asks the lady-in-the-tube-room, "Do you happen to have *Alice in Wonderland*?"

"Yes, we do! It's first on our shelf."

"Cool!" MH says. "I'm ready now, Mama."

Mama and I continue to stand in the doorway as MH jumps onto the sliding table. "Look, Mama. I get to go into the hole just like Alice!"

"You're going to have an adventure, Savannah!" The lady-in-the-tube-room says. Then she asks Mama, "*You* ready?"

Mama is not ready. I can feel it. I'm not ready either. But the lady-in-the-tube-room gets cheerful again and points to a chair in the other room, beyond the glass. Mama doesn't move.

"She's got this. She's very brave," the lady-in-the-tube-room says.

"Love you, Savanner-Danner-Doo," Mama calls out. "'Angels all around,' right?"

MH shouts back, "'For he will command his angels to guard you in all your ways,'" MH places the headphones over her ears and squeezes her eyes shut. "'In all *your* ways' too, Mama!" she shouts as she lies

down on the table.

Mama and I back out of the doorway. The lady-in-the-tube-room slides MH into the tube, then shuts the door. There's a window, so I stand on my hind feet to make sure the tube is behaving itself. Mama sits and motions for me to join her. Reluctantly, I lie at Mama's feet.

I hear the tube start up. Mama doesn't look up from her phone. They were right—the tube is quieter today, but I still want to bite it. I'm not allowed to bite, but if I were, I would bite that tube. Instead, I lay my head on Mama's foot as the tube begins to beep and clonk.

"BrrrRRRRRrrr BrrrRRRRRrrr BrrrRRRRRrrr BrrrRRRRRrrr BrrrRRRRRrrr," the tube says. "BeebooBeebooBeeBooBeebooBeeboo-BeeBooBeebooBeebooBeeBoo!"

Mama scratches my head. Twenty minutes is a long time for humans. But, it's a very, very, very long time for dogs.

"Beeb Beeb Beeb Beeb Beeb Beeb Beeb Beeb Beeb Beeb Beeb Beeb Beeb Beeb Beeb Beeb!"

A very, very, very, very, very, very, verrrrrrrry long time.

Finally, it stops, and there is silence. I lift my head.

I hear MH shout from the other room, "Out, out. Out now! Now!"

"Yes, out," the lady-in-the-tube-room agrees. "Slowly, though! We need to be safe!"

"I'm safe, I'm safe, I'm safe."

"There you go."

"I'm out! Yeah, Mama! I'm out!"

The lady-in-the-tube-room laughs. "Awesome job! Can I get a high-five?"

"First, Abby, please," MH says. "Abby and Mama."

"Of course. You stay right there while I open the door. Then I'll help you sit up."

Mama leads me into the room with the tube. I still want to bite it, but I'm not allowed to bite.

"Sit, Abby," Mama says, and I do. Then I watch the lady-in-the-tube-room help MH off the table.

"High-five," MH says to the lady-in-the-tube-room, then she smacks her hand. MH has wobbly legs. Mama helps her walk.

"Abby, come," Mama says.

Together we walk out of there, and Mama sits MH in a chair. I jump up on the chair beside her and place my paws on her shoulders. I press the side of my head against the side of her head. MH wraps her arms around me and holds me tight. *I sure needed this,* I think to myself. *I sure did.*

"Mama," MH says very softly.

"Yes, baby," Mama answers.

"I was very brave today."

"Yes, you were. Very brave."

"I stayed in the tube without the sleepy medicine. I stayed in the tube all by myself, Mama!"

"Yes, you did. You are my brave Warrior Princess."

I press my head firmer against MH's head and think to myself, *You are my brave Warrior Princess, too.*

"Mama," MH says softly.

"Yes, baby."

"I'm ready for some cheese, please!"

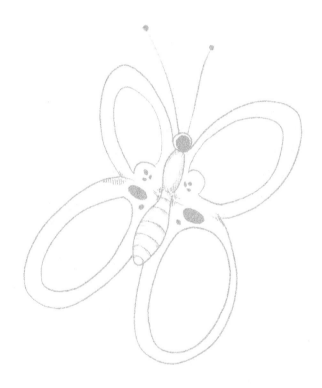

7

My Hero

Saturday

The house is quiet. MH gets to sleep in after all of the excitement of yesterday. So, we three are still lollygagging in Mama and Papa's bed. I don't know what *lollygag* means, except Papa says it when MH lays around in her pajamas until way past breakfast.

Mama woke up at her usual time and quietly slipped out of bed. I lifted my head to say 'good morning,' but she put her finger to her lips and said, "Shhhhhh." She rubbed my ears, then tiptoed into the kitchen to make MH a special treat. That's what happens whenever MH does something hard. Or scary. Or super hard and scary.

Mama slips back into bed, and now, she and I are watching MH sleep. Mama looks sad again, even though MH is calm and peaceful. She reaches over to touch MH like she's going to give her head a pet but then stops. Since MH is sleeping, Mama can't ask if a touch is okay. Mama looks at me and smiles a sad smile, her hand still hovering in the air. I lean my head toward her hand, so she doesn't waste a perfectly good head-pet. I am so relaxed that I let my eyes close for just a second. Then I hear a low rumble, like the sound Papa makes when he sleeps. I open my eyes to find MH watching me.

"You're snoring," she says to me. I find this hard to believe. She 'boops' my nose. "Mama, did we lollygag enough?"

Mama's phone makes the noise that means Papa is calling. All smiles now, Mama answers, "You need to confirm with Papa, but I think we broke our record!" She puts the phone up to her face. "Well! I'm sure I don't know who would call so early on a Saturday morning!"

"Early? Wake up, you lollygaggers!" MH scootches over so she can see Papa on the screen. "How are you, Danner-Doo?"

"Sleepy," she answers, followed by a big yawn and a stretch from the tips of her fingers to the tips of her toes. This gives Papa a case of the yawns. He stretches his arms high above his head as he scrunches his eyes shut, opens his mouth wide, makes a funny squeak noise, then lets all of his air out in a gush. "Made you yawn!" MH says through a fit of giggles. Mama hands her the phone, slips out of bed, and hurries to the kitchen.

"Yep, you did!" Papa agrees. "So, are you ready to get up and get moving?"

"No, Papa, I'm sleepy!"

"Not even for presents?"

"How? You're not here to give me presents."

"What happens after you do something scary and hard?"

"We lollygag, Mama makes cake pops, and you make me a treasure hunt."

"Right," Papa says. "Did Mama make cake pops?"

Sweeping back into the room, holding a treat out to MH, Mama says, "Of course, Mama made cake pops!" MH's eyes widen as she takes the treat and pokes the whole thing into her mouth.

"So," Papa says, "lollygagging, check. Hey! Are you eating that on *my* side of the bed?"

MH holds up an empty stick. Her cheeks bulge. "Cake pops, check!"

MH says, garbling her words. "But no treasure hunt," she adds, sounding a little sad.

"Oh, really?" Papa says, "Maybe you should check with Mama. She just might know where to find a list of clues." MH turns to Mama, who is holding out a piece of paper. MH bolts out of bed and down the hall. "Wait!" Papa shouts, "You need the list!"

"C'mon, Abby!" MH calls over her shoulder as she runs down into the room with the piles of laundry. I leap from the bed and chase her. She flings clothes into the air. A sock lands on my head. She digs to the bottom and pulls out a brand new book. "Yay! Math!" She rushes back to the bedroom with me close on her heels. She leaps back into bed. Out of breath, she says, "Oh, Papa, thank you! I filled up my other math workbook!"

"I know! You're welcome!"

Mama is still holding the note. "How did you know where to look?" she asks.

"Papa always hides things for me there. He says it's the perfect place 'cuz you can never see the floor."

"Oh, really?" Mama says, and one of her eyebrows goes way up.

MH takes the list from Mama's hand and reads: "'Second clue: It's in my shoe on the floor by the closet door.'" MH hops off the bed and looks in the closet to find one of Papa's golf shoes out of place. MH reaches for what's inside it. "Oh, boy! Mini Golf coupons! Thanks, Papa!"

"You're welcome, Danner-Doo. Now for this last one, you'll need Mama's help."

"Oh, okay. Ready, Mama?"

"Yep, I'm ready," she answers.

MH reads: "Third clue: It's in the place where Mama keeps her jewelry case."

Mama goes to the table where she puts on her makeup.

"Look in the top drawer of your vanity," Papa instructs. In the drawer are three little boxes with their names on top.

Mama brings them over to the bed and sits. "Savannah, will you open Mama's box, please?"

MH lifts the lid and takes out a shiny silver necklace. "It's a heart on an anchor," MH tells Mama as she hands it to her.

"Because Mama is the anchor for our love," Papa says, as tears spill out of Mama's eyes. "Now, Savannah, will you open Abby's box, please?" MH lifts the lid and takes out a shiny silver tag.

"It says, 'Wonder Dog,'" MH tells me.

"Because Abby is our trusty sidekick, always ready to save the day."

"Oh, Papa, it's perfect," MH says. "Abby, that's what you are—our Wonder Dog!"

"Yes, she is," Papa agrees. "I hope you all like your gifts. I miss you."

"Papa! It's my turn to open my box!"

"Oh, right," Papa jokes. "Savannah, will you open your box, please?"

She lifts the lid and takes out a shiny silver bracelet with words on it. "It says, 'Warrior. Princess. My Hero.' MH looks into the screen on Mama's phone and asks, "Me, Papa? A hero?"

"Without a doubt. You are the bravest person I know." Papa blows kisses before he has to end the call. Mama puts on her necklace. She wraps her fingers around the anchor with the heart and closes her eyes. MH slowly runs her finger across the letters of her new bracelet.

It's perfect, I think to myself. *That is what you are, MH—my Warrior Princess! My hero! The bravest person I know!!!*

The End

"So don't worry about tomorrow.
Each day has enough trouble of its own.
Tomorrow will have its own worries.

(Matthew 6:34)

"He has put his angels in charge of you.
They will watch over you wherever you go."

(Psalms 91:11)

ABOUT CLIMBING ANGEL PUBLISHING

Climbing Angel Publishing exists for the purpose of sharing stories of hope and encouragement, aiding in the gathering together of community, and supporting the process of betterment. The following books are available at ClimbingAngel.com and major bookstores.

ADULT BOOKS: (Romans 8:28-30)

In His Image, by Sam Polson (English, Romanian, & Mandarin)
By Faith, by Sam Polson (English & Romanian)
My Birthday Gift to Jesus, by Lisa Soland
Without Ceasing, by Dr. Dennis Davidson
SonLight: Daily Light from the Pages of God's Word, by Sam Polson
Corona Victus: Conquering the Virus of Fear, by Sam Polson
Art Bushing: His Diary, Letters, & Photographs of WWII, by Art Bushing
Art & Dotty: His Diary, Their Letters & Photographs of WWII by Art Bushing
Trimisul, by Stan Johnson (Romanian)
Life Changing Prayer, by Sam Polson
The Climbing Angel Christmas Treasury, by a variety of authors
J. Calvin Coolidge: Letters from the Korean War
Stories from Kingman, AZ: The Heart of Historic Route 66 by Loren B. Wilson
Pathways, by Sam Polson

CHILDREN'S BOOKS: (Philippians 4:8)

The Christmas Tree Angel, by Lisa Soland
The Unmade Moose, by Lisa Soland
Thump, by Lisa Soland
Somebunny To Love, by Lisa Soland (English & Mandarin)
The Truth About God's Rainbow, by Lisa Soland
God's Promises, by Lisa Soland
The Boy & The Bagel Necklace, by Lisa Soland
God's Hands and Feet, by Lisa Soland
I Like To Be Quiet, by Joni Caldwell
Wheels Off!, by Karlie Saumier

Ella's Trip of a Lifetime, by Melanie Ewbank
You Are Mine, by Gayle Childress Greene
Jeremy Plays the Blues, by Amy Oden Simpson
Bad Hair Day, by Jasmyne Simpkins
I Like To Read, by Joni Caldwell
Trunks Up!, by Karlie Saumier
Perusha's Paradise, by Bette Reed Smith
Ruby and the Treasure Within, by Tonya Celeste Hobbs
Abby, the Wonder Dog and her Warrior Princess by Melanie Ewbank